D1576320

913 000 00019376

LONDON BOROUGH OF HACKNEY	
913 000 00019376	
HJ	30-Oct-2009
JF	£5.99

First published 2009 by Walker Books Ltd
87 Vauxhall Walk, London SE11 5HJ

2 4 6 8 10 9 7 5 3 1

© 2009 John Lechner

The right of John Lechner to be identified as
author/illustrator of this work has been asserted by him in
accordance with the Copyright, Designs and Patents Act 1988

This book has been typeset in Journal.

Printed in China

All rights reserved. No part of this book may be reproduced,
transmitted or stored in an information retrieval system
in any form or by any means, graphic, electronic or
mechanical, including photocopying, taping and recording,
without prior written permission from the publisher.

British Library Cataloguing in Publication Data:
a catalogue record for this book is available from the British
Library

ISBN 978-1-4063-2223-1

www.walker.co.uk

The Clever Stick

John Lechner

WALKER BOOKS
AND SUBSIDIARIES

LONDON · BOSTON · SYDNEY · AUCKLAND

Once upon a time, there
was a clever stick.

Ever since he fell
off the tree he'd
been sharp.

He would sit in the
forest and think all
sorts of clever things.

He would float down the stream, making up poetry.

He would listen to the singing
of the birds and wonder what
made it sound so beautiful.

But the poor stick
had one problem ...
he couldn't speak.

So he couldn't share
his thoughts with the
other forest creatures.

When he saw chipmunks gathering food, he wanted to tell them, "I know somewhere you can find lots of acorns."

But he kept silent. Who would believe a stick anyway?

When he came across a frog writing a poem, he wanted to share a simile about the sun being like a dragon.

But he couldn't.

And when he saw a wild rose growing
in a field, he longed to tell her how
beautiful she was.

But he could only remain silent.

One bright day as the stick approached
the meadow, he tried to say hello to
all the animals, insects and flowers by
bowing deeply ...

but he tripped on a pebble and fell
flat on his face.

Nobody even noticed.

The clever stick
didn't feel so
clever any more.

He dragged himself
all the way home.

When finally he stopped, he noticed
the trail he had left in the earth.

It looked interesting so he
made some more lines.

To his amazement, he discovered that he could draw lines to look like things.

The stick began to draw vigorously
in the earth. A giant tapestry emerged
from the dust.

As he scribbled, the plants, animals
and insects gathered round and
watched intently.

But the stick didn't even notice.
He drew faster and faster.

Finally he stopped. The dust cleared ...

and there was the most magnificent
sight the forest had ever seen.

The animals cheered, the insects buzzed and the trees swayed their branches in approval.

Even the rose turned
her petals to look.

All of a sudden, a drop of water fell
from the sky ... then another.

The animals scattered, the plants closed their leaves, and in minutes the stick's masterpiece had washed away.

But the stick was not upset. He
knew he could make another ...

he knew at last he had
found his voice.

But right now he didn't want to
get wet.

So he took a fallen leaf and made himself an umbrella.

He truly was a
clever stick, you see.